Inky
the Indigo
Fairy

Special thanks to
Narinder Dhami

ISBN-13: 978-0-439-74685-4
ISBN-10: 0-439-74685-X

12 11 10 9   10 11 12/0

Printed in China

Inky
the Indigo
Fairy

by Daisy Meadows
illustrated by Georgie Ripper

SCHOLASTIC INC.

New York   Toronto   London   Auckland   Sydney
Mexico City   New Delhi   Hong Kong   Buenos Aires

The Fairyland Palace

Maze

Forest

Black Pot

Orchard

Meadow

Tower

Beach

Rock pools

Rainspell Island

Cold winds blow and thick ice forms,
I conjure up this fairy storm.
To seven corners of the human world
the Rainbow Fairies will be hurled!

I curse every part of Fairyland,
with a frosty wave of my icy hand.
For now and always, from this day,
Fairyland will be cold and gray!

Ruby, Amber, Sunny, Fern, and Sky
are all safe and sound. Now Rachel
and Kirsty must find
Inky the Indigo Fairy!
But is she in trouble?

Contents

A Fairy-tale Beginning

"Rain, rain, go away," Rachel Walker said with a sigh. "Come again another day!"

She and her friend Kirsty Tate stared out of the attic window. Raindrops splashed against the glass, and the sky was full of purplish-black clouds.

"Isn't it a terrible day outside?" Kirsty said. "But it's nice and cozy in here."

1

She looked around Rachel's small attic
bedroom. There was just enough room for
a brass bed with a patchwork quilt, a
comfy armchair, and an old bookshelf.

"But you know what the weather
on Rainspell Island is like," Rachel
pointed out. "It could be hot and sunny
very soon!"

Both girls had come to Rainspell Island
on vacation. The Walkers were staying in
Mermaid Cottage, while the Tates were
in Dolphin Cottage next door.

Kirsty frowned. "Yes, but what about Inky the Indigo Fairy?" she asked. "We have to find her today."

Rachel and Kirsty shared a wonderful secret. They were trying to find the seven Rainbow Fairies, who had been cast out of Fairyland by mean Jack Frost. Fairyland would be cold and gray until all seven fairies had been found again.

Rachel thought of Ruby, Amber, Sunny, Fern, and Sky, who were all safe now in the pot at the end of the rainbow. Only Inky the Indigo Fairy and Heather the Violet Fairy were left to find. But how could the girls look for them while they were stuck indoors?

"Remember what the Fairy Queen said?" Rachel reminded Kirsty.

Kirsty nodded. "She said the magic would come to us." Suddenly, she looked scared. "Maybe the rain is Jack Frost's magic. What if he's trying to stop us from finding Inky?"

"Oh, no!" Rachel said. "Let's hope the rain stops soon. But what should we do while we wait?"

Kirsty thought for a minute. Then she walked over to the bookshelf. It was filled with dusty old books that looked like

they hadn't been read in a long time. She pulled one out. It was so big that Kirsty had to use two hands to hold it. "*The Big Book of Fairy Tales*," Rachel read out loud, looking at the cover.

"If we can't find fairies today, at least we can read about them!" Kirsty grinned.

The two girls sat down on the bed and put the book on their knees. Kirsty was about to turn to the first page when Rachel gasped. "Kirsty, look at the cover! It's purple. A really deep purplish-blue."

"That's indigo," Kirsty whispered. "Oh, Rachel! Do you think Inky could be trapped inside?"

"Let's see," Rachel said. "Hurry up, Kirsty. Open the book!"

But Kirsty had spotted something else. "Rachel," she said. "It's *glowing*."

Rachel looked more closely. Kirsty was right! Some pages in the middle of the book were shining with a soft bluish-purple light.

Kirsty opened the book. The ink on the pages was glowing indigo, too. For a minute, Kirsty thought that Inky might fly right out of the pages, but there was no sign of her. On the first page of the book was a picture of a wooden soldier. Above the picture were the words: *The Nutcracker.*

"Oh!" Rachel said. "I know this story. I went to see the ballet at Christmas."

"What's it about?" Kirsty asked.

"Well, a girl named Clara gets a wooden nutcracker soldier for Christmas," Rachel explained. "He comes to life and takes her to the Land of Sweets." They looked in the book and saw a colored picture of a Christmas tree. A little girl was asleep next to it, holding a wooden soldier.

On the next page there was a picture of snowflakes whirling and swirling through a dark forest. "Aren't the pictures great?" Kirsty said. "The snow looks so real."

Rachel frowned. For just a minute, she thought the snowflakes were moving. Gently, she put out her hand and touched the page. It felt cold and wet!

"Kirsty," she whispered. "It *is* real!" She held out her hand. There were white snowflakes on her fingers.

Kirsty looked down at the book again, her eyes wide. Just then, the snowflakes started to swirl from the book's pages, right into the bedroom. They moved slowly at first, then faster and faster. Soon the snowstorm was so thick, Rachel and Kirsty couldn't see a thing. But they could feel themselves being swept up into the air by the spinning cloud of snow.

Rachel yelled to Kirsty, "Why haven't we hit the bedroom ceiling?"

Kirsty reached for Rachel's hand and held on tight. "Because it's magic!" she replied.

The Land of Sweets

Suddenly, the snowflakes stopped
swirling. Rachel and Kirsty found
themselves standing in a forest, with their
backpacks at their feet. Tall trees towered
around them and crisp white snow
covered the ground. The girls certainly
weren't in Rachel's bedroom anymore.

Then Rachel realized where they were.

"Kirsty, this is the forest that was in the picture," she said, grabbing her friend's arm. "We're *inside* the book!"

Kirsty looked frightened. "Do you think Jack Frost brought us here?" she asked. "Or his goblins?" Jack Frost's goblins were always trying to keep Rachel and Kirsty from finding the Rainbow Fairies.

"I don't know," Rachel replied. Then she frowned. There was something strange about this snow. She bent down and gently touched a snowdrift.

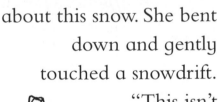

"This isn't snow." Rachel laughed. "It's powdered sugar!"

"What?" Kirsty looked amazed. She scooped up a handful and tasted it. The powdered sugar was cool and sweet.

"Maybe this isn't Jack Frost's magic after all," Rachel said.

"What's that?" Kirsty asked, pointing.

Rachel could see a pink and gold glow coming through the trees. "Let's go find out," she said.

The girls picked up their backpacks

and headed toward the glow. It was hard
walking through the powdered sugar.
Soon their sneakers were covered in the
sugary snow.

Crack!

Rachel jumped as a loud noise echoed
through the trees.

"Sorry," said Kirsty. "I stepped on a stick."

"Wait," Rachel whispered. "I just heard
voices!"

"Do you think it could be goblins?"
Kirsty whispered back, looking scared
again.

Rachel listened. The voices were louder now. She sighed with relief. "No, they sound too sweet to be goblins' voices."

Rachel and Kirsty hurried toward the edge of the forest. When they came out of the trees, they saw that the glow was coming from a beautiful pink and gold archway.

"Look, Kirsty," Rachel gasped. "It's made of candy!"

Kirsty stared. The archway was made of pink marshmallows and golden caramel.

Then the girls heard the voices again, and they spun around. Two people dressed in fluffy, white coats were talking to each other and scooping powdered sugar into shiny metal buckets. They had round, rosy cheeks and small, pointy ears. They were so busy that they hadn't noticed Rachel or Kirsty yet.

"I think they're elves!" Kirsty whispered. "But they're the same size as we are. That means we must be fairy-sized again."

"We don't have any wings this time, though," Rachel whispered back.

Suddenly, one of the elves spotted them. She looked very surprised. "Hello!" she called. "Where did you come from?"

"I'm Rachel and this is Kirsty," Rachel explained. "We came here through the forest."

"Where are we?" Kirsty asked.

"This is the entrance to the Land of Sweets," said the first elf. "My name is Wafer, and this is my sister, Cone."

"We're the ice-cream makers," added Cone. "What are you doing here?"

"We're looking for Inky the Indigo Fairy," Kirsty told them. "Have you seen her?"

Both elves shook their heads. "We've heard of the Rainbow Fairies," said Wafer. "But Fairyland is far away, across the Lemonade Ocean."

"Maybe you should ask the Sugarplum Fairy for help," Cone said. "She's so smart, she'll know what to do. She lives on the other side of the village."

"Could you take us to her?" Rachel asked eagerly.

The elves nodded. "Follow us," they

said together. Then they led Rachel and Kirsty through the candy archway.

On the other side of the arch, the sun shone down warmly from a bright blue sky. Flowers made of whipped cream grew underneath chocolate trees. Squishy pink and white marshmallow houses lined the street, which was paved with jelly beans.

"Isn't this great?" Kirsty laughed. "It's like being inside a giant candy store!"

"And it all looks *yummy!*" Rachel agreed.

There were elves everywhere! Some had shiny buckets like the ice-cream makers, and others carried tiny, silver hammers. There were gingerbread men, too, looking very stylish in their bright bow ties and chocolate buttons. Then a whole line of tiny wooden soldiers in polished black boots marched across the street in front of them, and Rachel spotted a sparkling pink sugar mouse scurrying between their feet. Kirsty and Rachel smiled at each other. What a fun place this was!

The two elves led Rachel and Kirsty
down the street. Suddenly, an angry-
looking gingerbread man hurried out of
one of the houses and bumped into Cone.

"Hello, Buttons," Wafer said. "Are you
in a hurry?"

"What's the matter?" Cone asked. "You
look upset."

The gingerbread man
held out his hand. "Look
at my best bow tie!" he
said. "It was red when I hung it
out to dry, and now it's *this* color!"

Rachel and Kirsty gasped. The bow tie was purplish-blue!

"Inky!" they both said together.

The ice-cream elves looked confused.

"I think this means that Inky the Indigo Fairy is close by," Rachel explained.

"We'd better help you find her before she causes any more trouble," Cone said. Then she frowned as a small boy elf ran toward them. He had one hand over his mouth, and he was laughing.

"Scoop!" called Wafer. She turned to Rachel and Kirsty. "He's our little brother," she explained. "Scoop, what are you giggling about?"

Still laughing, Scoop took his hand away from his mouth. Rachel and Kirsty stared. The little elf's mouth was stained indigo!

"What happened?" Cone gasped.

"I had a drink from the lemonade fountain," Scoop said between giggles. "All the lemonade is a purplish-blue color. It made my tongue tingle, too!"

"That sounds like more Rainbow Fairy magic!" Kirsty said.

"Where's the lemonade fountain?"
Rachel asked the elves.

"In the village square," replied Cone.
"Just around the corner."

"Thanks for your help," said Kirsty.
She grabbed Rachel's hand and they
ran off.

As soon as Rachel and Kirsty turned
around the corner, they skidded to a halt.
In the middle of the village square was a
pretty fountain. Bright purplish-blue
liquid bubbled up from a fountain shaped
like a dolphin. A crowd of elves, soldiers,
and gingerbread men stood around the
fountain. They were all talking at once,
and they sounded angry! A polka-dotted
jack-in-the-box bounced back and forth
with a grumpy look on his face.

A swirl of indigo fairy dust shot up from the middle of the crowd. As the dust fell to the ground, it changed into blackberry-scented ink drops.

Rachel and Kirsty stared at each other. Fairy dust could only mean one thing. They had found another Rainbow Fairy!

Look Out!

"Inky!" Rachel called as she and Kirsty pushed their way through the crowd. "Is that you?"

"Who's that?" called a tiny voice.

Inky was standing by the edge of the lemonade fountain. She had neat blue-black hair and twinkling, dark blue eyes.

She was dressed in indigo jeans and a
matching jacket that were covered with
sparkly patches. Her wand was indigo,
tipped with silver.

The fairy stared at Rachel and Kirsty
with her hands on her hips. "Who are
you?" she asked. "And how do you know
my name?"

"I'm Kirsty, and this is Rachel," Kirsty
explained. "We've come to take you back
to your Rainbow sisters."

"We've found five of your sisters so far,"
Rachel added. "We're going to help you
all go home to Fairyland."

"That's wonderful news!" Inky
cried. "I've been so
worried about them."

"How did you get
to the Land of
Sweets?" Kirsty
asked.

"The wind blew me
down the chimney of
Mermaid Cottage, and
into the *The Nutcracker*
book," Inky replied. "I've been
in the Land of Sweets ever since. But I
can't go back to Fairyland and break
Jack Frost's spell without my sisters. I have
to get back to Rainspell Island first."

Before Rachel and Kirsty could say anything else, the crowd started shouting again.

"Look what she did to the lemonade  fountain!" grumbled one elf. Inky grinned at him. "I didn't mean to," she said. "The lemonade looked so yummy, I just had to take a drink. And that's when it turned indigo."

"And what about my bow tie?" snapped Buttons. He had followed Kirsty and Rachel to the fountain.

"I was really tired after walking through the forest," Inky explained. "I used your bow tie as a pillow while I took a little nap."

The crowd started to mutter angrily again.

Quickly, Rachel stepped forward.
"Wait," she said. "Have you all heard
about the Rainbow Fairies and Jack
Frost's spell?"

The crowd listened as Rachel told them
the whole story. When she'd finished, they
didn't look angry anymore.

"I'm *so* sorry for all the trouble I've
caused," Inky said. "Can you please tell
us how to get back to Rainspell Island?"

"The Sugarplum Fairy can help you," said the jack-in-the-box, with a little bounce. "Her home is just past the jelly bean fields."

"That's where we were going," Kirsty said.

"Come on, then!" Inky cried. She jumped forward and took Rachel and Kirsty by the hand.

"Good luck!" everyone called.

Rachel and Kirsty walked along the
road toward the jelly bean fields while
Inky darted out eagerly ahead of them.
Just outside the village was a huge rock
made of hardened caramel. It was as tall
as a marshmallow house! Elves were
tapping the rock with little hammers to
break off pieces. Other elves picked up the
pieces and put them into silver buckets.

Kirsty nudged Rachel. "That looks like hard work," she said. "They don't seem to be collecting much caramel at all!"

Rachel peeked into one of the buckets as an elf walked past. Kirsty was right. There were only a few chips of caramel in it.

"Is there something wrong with the caramel?" Inky wondered.

The elf with the bucket overheard her. "It's really hard today," he grumbled. "It almost seems like it has been *frozen*."

"Frozen!" Kirsty said in alarm. "Do you think that means Jack Frost's goblins are here, in the Land of Sweets?" The girls knew that whenever the goblins were close by, they brought frost and icy weather.

Inky looked scared. "I hope not,"
she said.

Just then, a loud, rumbling noise made
them all jump. "Look out!" someone
cried. An enormous wooden barrel was
rolling down the street, right toward
them! And running behind it were two
goblins with big, mean grins on their faces.

Stop Those Goblins!

"We've got you now, Inky!" shouted one of the goblins.

For a minute everyone froze. Then Inky leaped into action and gave Rachel and Kirsty a push. "Quick! Get out of the way!" she yelled.

The girls jumped aside just in time. The elves dropped their hammers and buckets.

They ran out of the way, too, bumping into one another in their panic.

Crash!

The barrel smashed right into the caramel mountain. Then it cracked open. Cocoa powder spilled out in a sticky brown cloud.

"Inky! Kirsty!" Rachel coughed, digging her way through the cocoa. "Are you OK?"

"I think so!" Kirsty sneezed. *"Achoo!"*

"HELP!"

Kirsty heard Inky's frightened voice. But she couldn't see her through the cocoa cloud.

"Help!" Inky shouted again. "The goblins got me!" Her voice was getting fainter.

"Quick, Rachel!" Kirsty said. "Do you have our magic bags?"

Still coughing, Rachel swung her backpack around. Titania, the Fairy Queen, had given the girls bags full of magic gifts to help them rescue the missing Rainbow Fairies.

Rachel opened her backpack. Inside it, one of the magic bags was glowing. Rachel pulled out a folded paper fan from the bag. Puzzled, she opened the fan. It looked like the most beautiful

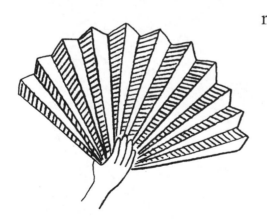

rainbow she had ever seen, with stripes of red, orange, yellow, green, blue, indigo, and violet.

Rachel thought for a minute. Then she began to flap the fan at the clouds of cocoa.

Whoosh!

A blast of air from the fan blew almost all of the cocoa away.

"Wow! This fan is amazing!" Rachel said as the last of the cocoa drifted off.

"Look, Rachel!" shouted Kirsty. "They're over there!"

The goblins had tied Inky's sneakers together with strawberry licorice. They were dragging her up the road, toward the jelly bean fields.

"We've got to save her," Rachel said, quickly folding the fan and putting it in her pocket. "Come on, Kirsty!"

"I'll go tell the Sugarplum Fairy," said one of the elves, and he ran off in the other direction.

Rachel and Kirsty ran up the road after Inky. The goblins had a head start, but Inky was wriggling and squirming so much that she was slowing them down.

The road led right through the jelly bean fields. Tall green plants stood in rows, each one covered with different-colored beans — pink, white, blue-spotted, and chocolate-brown ones. Elves were picking the jelly beans and putting them into big baskets.

Suddenly, Rachel noticed that the goblins were looking greedily at the jelly beans as they ran by with Inky. One of them skidded to a halt. He leaned over the fence and grabbed a big jelly bean from the nearest plant. The other goblin did the same.

"Yummy!" said the first goblin, stuffing the bean into his mouth.

"They're so greedy!" Rachel panted.

"Yes, but it gives me an idea of how to trick them!" Kirsty puffed. She started to run even faster.

The elves working in the field yelled at the goblins. But that didn't stop them. They gobbled down one bean after another. They picked beans with one hand and held on to Inky with the other.

44

"I have an idea," Rachel whispered to Kirsty. On one side of the road she could see some baskets full of jelly beans that had already been picked. She hurried over and grabbed a basket. Then she held it out toward the goblins.

"Look what I have," she called. "A whole basketful of beans!"

A Perfect Punishment

The goblins' eyes lit up
when they saw the basket. Inky
grinned and winked at Kirsty and
Rachel. She knew what they were
doing.

"Those jelly beans look yummy,"
Inky said to the goblins. "I wish I
could have one."

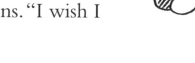

"Be quiet," snapped the goblin with the bigger nose. He turned to the other goblin. "You hang on to the fairy while I get the beans."

"No," said the other one. "You'll eat them all! You hold the fairy, and *I'll* get the beans."

"No!" roared the first goblin. "Then *you'll* eat all the beans!"

Glaring at each other, both goblins let go of Inky and ran toward Rachel.

She quickly threw an armful of beans

on the ground and backed away. The goblins bent down to grab the beans. When they stood up again, Rachel threw another armful back down the hill, away from Inky.

Those greedy goblins just couldn't resist the yummy jelly beans!

While the goblins were busy stuffing themselves, Kirsty rushed over to untie Inky. "Are you all right?" she asked.

Inky nodded and wriggled her feet free from the licorice ropes. "Thank you!"

Rachel put the basket on the ground and ran over to Kirsty and Inky. The goblins pounced on the basket and began arguing over the rest of the jelly beans.

"Let's get out of here before they realize that Inky is free!" Rachel said.

Suddenly, there was a gentle flapping noise overhead. Rachel looked up to see a huge butterfly with pink and gold wings fluttering above them. On its back sat a fairy with long, red hair.

The butterfly landed lightly on the ground. The fairy climbed off the butterfly's back and smiled at Inky and the girls. She wore a long green and gold dress and a tiara.

"Hello," she said. "I am the Sugarplum Fairy." She looked sternly at the goblins who were crouching beside the empty jelly bean basket. "What are *you* doing in the Land of Sweets?" she demanded.

The goblins didn't answer. They were too busy groaning and holding their stomachs.

"Oooh!" moaned the goblin with the big nose. "My tummy hurts."

"Mine, too," whined the other one. "I feel sick."

"They ate too many jelly beans!" Inky said, grinning at Rachel and Kirsty.

The Sugarplum Fairy looked even angrier. "You must be taught a lesson," she said to the goblins, "since you have stolen so many of our delicious jelly beans."

"Why don't you make them pick more jelly beans?" Inky suggested.

"What a good idea." The Sugarplum Fairy smiled.

"That doesn't seem like a very bad punishment," Kirsty whispered to Rachel.

"But just look at the goblins' faces," Rachel whispered back.

The goblins looked horrified at the
thought of more jelly beans! They tried to
get up, like they wanted to run away. But
the Sugarplum Fairy waved her hand
and a few elves came running out of the
jelly bean fields. They marched the
goblins into the nearest field and handed
them empty baskets. With sulky faces, the
goblins started to pick the jelly beans.

"Serves them right!" Inky laughed. Then she looked worried again. "But I still need to get back to my Rainbow sisters."

"Please, can you help us get back to Rainspell Island?" Rachel asked the Sugarplum Fairy. "We would use fairy magic to fly back, but we don't know how to get there!"

The beautiful fairy nodded. "We will send you home by balloon!" she said. She waved her wand at the empty jelly bean basket. Rachel and Kirsty watched in amazement as it grew bigger and bigger. "But where's the balloon?" asked Rachel.

The Sugarplum
Fairy pointed to a
tall tree, covered with
pink blossoms.

"What pretty flowers,"
Kirsty said. Then she took
a closer look and began to laugh.
"They're not flowers. They're pieces of
bubble gum!"

"How is that going to help?" Rachel
was confused.

Inky grinned at them, her eyes
sparkling mischievously.
"Leave it to me!" she said.
She pulled one of the
bubble-gum flowers off
the tree, popped it
into her mouth, and
began to chew.

Then, squeezing her eyes
shut tight, Inky blew a
huge, purplish-blue
bubble. She puffed
and puffed,
and the bubble
grew bigger and
bigger. Soon, it towered
above them. It was
the biggest bubble
Rachel and Kirsty

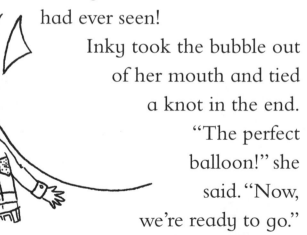

had ever seen!
Inky took the bubble out
of her mouth and tied
a knot in the end.
"The perfect
balloon!" she
said. "Now,
we're ready to go."

Rachel and Kirsty grinned at each
other. What a wonderful
way to travel back to
Rainspell Island!

The elves
helped tie the
bubble-gum
balloon to the
basket. Then,
Rachel,
Kirsty, and
Inky climbed
inside.

The
Sugarplum
Fairy waved
her wand at the
balloon, showering it
with gold sparkles.

"The balloon will take you back to Rainspell Island," she explained.

"Good-bye, and good luck."

"Thank you," called Rachel and Inky.

But Kirsty was looking around in dismay. "There's no wind!" she said. "We won't be able to get off the ground!"

The Bubble-gum Balloon

Rachel looked over at the leaves on the
bubble-gum tree. Kirsty was right. They
weren't moving at all!

The Sugarplum Fairy smiled. "Rachel,
don't you remember what you have in
your pocket?" she said.

"Of course!" Rachel exclaimed. "The
magic fan!" She took it out of her pocket

and unfolded it. Then, she flapped it
under the balloon.

Whoosh!

The blast of air lifted the balloon up
into the sky. "Good-bye!"
Kirsty called, waving at the
Sugarplum Fairy and all
the elves.

"Thank you for all
your help," Inky
said. "Sorry I made
such a mess!" she
added with a giggle.

The balloon bobbed
slowly upward. As it got
higher, the wind became
stronger, so Rachel put the fan back
in her pocket. Big, puffy clouds began
swirling around the balloon.

"We'll be home soon," Rachel said, trying to sound cheerful.

The wind roared around them, rocking the basket from side to side. Rachel, Kirsty, and Inky hung on to one another and squeezed their eyes shut.

Then, all of a sudden, the wind dropped. The balloon stopped swaying. The air felt warm.

Kirsty opened her eyes. "We're home!" she gasped.

They were back in Rachel's attic
bedroom at Mermaid Cottage. The
balloon and the basket had vanished. The
book of fairy tales was lying on the floor,
open to *The Nutcracker*.

"But where's Inky?" Rachel said.

"I'm in here!" said a small, cheerful voice. The Indigo Fairy popped up from Rachel's pocket. She wriggled out and fluttered into the air, her wings sparkling with rainbows and showering the room with fairy dust ink drops. The smell of blackberries filled the air as they popped.

Kirsty picked up the book. She turned the pages until she found a picture of the Land of Sweets. "It's a shame we didn't get to taste any of that wonderful candy," she said.

As she spoke, a tiny puff of powdered sugar floated out of the book. Then, a shower of different-colored jelly beans fell onto Rachel's bed.

"They must be a present from the Sugarplum Fairy!" Inky laughed.

Rachel and Kirsty each popped a jelly bean into their mouth. They were tiny, but they tasted delicious!

"Yum!" said Inky, munching a bean. "Can we take some back to the pot for my sisters?"

Rachel nodded. "Let's go right away," she said, filling her pockets with jelly beans. "Your sisters will be waiting for you." She looked at Kirsty and smiled. They had escaped the goblins and rescued another fairy. They'd even been inside a fairy tale. And, now, there was only one more fairy to find! Rachel and Kirsty were so close to bringing the color back to Fairyland, they could almost taste it!

THE RAINBOW FAIRIES

Only one Rainbow Fairy is still missing!
Fairyland will never get its Rainbow
Magic back without

Heather the Violet Fairy!

But where is the final fairy?
Join Kirsty and Rachel's adventure in
this special sneak peek. . . .

Message on a Kite

"I can't believe this is the last day of our vacation!" said Rachel Walker. She gazed up at her kite as it rose in the clear blue sky.

Kirsty Tate watched the purple kite soar above the field next to Mermaid Cottage. "But we still have to find Heather the Violet Fairy!" she reminded Rachel.

Mean Jack Frost had cast a wicked spell that banished the seven Rainbow Fairies to Rainspell Island. And without the Rainbow Fairies, Fairyland had no color! Kirsty and Rachel had already found Ruby, Amber, Sunny, Fern, Sky, and Inky. Now they only had Heather the Violet Fairy left to find.

Rachel felt the kite tug on its string. She looked up. Something violet and silver flashed at the end of the kite's long tail. "Look up there!" she shouted.

Kirsty shaded her eyes with her hand. "What is it? Do you think it's a fairy?" she asked.

"I'm not sure," Rachel said, winding in the string.

As the kite came bobbing toward them, Kirsty saw that a long piece of violet-colored ribbon was tied to its tail. She helped Rachel untie the ribbon and smooth it out.

"It has tiny silver writing on it," Rachel gasped.

Read the rest of

THE RAINBOW FAIRIES

Heather the Violet Fairy
to find out what's
written on the shiny ribbon.

Can Rachel and Kirsty track
down the final fairy?

RAINBOW magic™

There's Magic in Every Series!

The Rainbow Fairies

The Weather Fairies

The Jewel Fairies

The Pet Fairies

The Fun Day Fairies

The Petal Fairies

The Dance Fairies

The Music Fairies

The Sports Fairies

The Party Fairies

Read them all!

SCHOLASTIC

www.scholastic.com

www.rainbowmagiconline.com

HIT entertainment

RMFAIRY2